THE
DEAD
DETECTIVE

in

DEAD LOSS

by Felix Bogarte™

Published 2003 by Books Noir Ltd, Glasgow

Copyright © 2003 Books Noir Ltd

Text written by Joan Love and Mhairi MacDiarmid,
based on a story by Mhairi MacDiarmid

A CIP catalogue for this book is available from the British Library

ISBN 1-904684-02-5

Printed and bound in the EU

www.booksnoir.com
www.deaddetective.com
info@deaddetective.com

CONTENTS

WHO'S WHO IN
DEAD DETECTIVE LAND

WHO IS CHARLIE CHRISTIAN?

12 year-old Charlie Christian is a born detective – and has been given the opportunity to prove himself. The Court Of Ghouls, who exist in a twilight zone between life and death have decreed that the Dead Detective, Hank Kane be sentenced to fight crime in Charlie's very own city of Glasgow! And, as Hank Kane cannot be trusted to solve cases honestly he has been instructed to take on someone he can train as a detective – someone like Charlie Christian.

WHO IS ANNIE?

Ten year-old Annie, or "Ace" as her brother, Charlie, insists on calling her is the world's most reluctant detective. To say that she doesn't share her brother's love of all things detective would be putting it mildly – the whole investigative "scene" bores her senseless.

WHO IS THE GRIM REAPER?

The Grim Reaper, or TG as he likes to be known,

really enjoys his work. He loves the perks of his job, annoying Hank, partying and fiddling his expenses.

SO, WHO IS THE DEAD DETECTIVE?

The Dead Detective is Hank Kane, a crooked cop, killed in the line of duty in Los Angeles in the 1950s. Instead of passing straight over to the other side, however, Hank finds himself facing the Court Of Ghouls, who have decided that he'll have to pay for his habit of planting evidence on suspects. They sentence him to fighting crime, using only honest methods, until they are convinced that he's learnt his lesson. They instruct The Grim Reaper to keep an eye on Hank. It isn't that they don't totally trust Hank – it's just that they don't trust him at all!

Hank's other problem is his appearance. He's a skeleton! During daylight hours he has no flesh on his bones (well, he *is* dead!) and so has to stay out of sight. At night, however, providing he drinks some of his chemical compound, flesh returns to his bones and he looks almost normal. "Almost" because Hank died fifty years previously and has been catapulted forward in time to 2003.

CHAPTER ONE
AN OLD FRIEND

HANK Kane leaned back in his office chair, stretched and yawned. He reached over and turned off his desk lamp, glancing at the empty coffee cup lying beside the half eaten biscuit. He shrugged. He'd clear it away in the morning; the thought of taking them into the tiny kitchen seemed like a supreme effort right now. He just felt too goddamn tired.

He dragged himself towards his bedroom where the small bedside lamp cast an eerie glow around the room. Hank caught sight of his reflection in the mirror. He looked paler than ever and that was saying something.

He pulled the covers back from the bed and then stopped. He could hear someone in his office. TG maybe? He listened more intently. It sounded like someone knocking on the office door.

Hank made his way over to the door, looking around for TG. There was no sign of him. He unlocked the door and looked outside into the hallway but it was empty. Strange. He closed the door and locked it again.

As he was about to go back into his bedroom, he heard the noise again. It was a loud, tapping noise. This time it was more clear and more insistent. It was coming from the opposite end of the room. The window. He moved, more quickly this time and pulled up the blind.

He couldn't see anything at first as his eyes were unaccustomed to the darkness. He blinked and was gradually able to make out a face. It was a man's face and his hand was tapping insistently on the glass.

Hank pulled the blind up as far as it would go and lifted up the window. He looked at he man curiously.

"It's me, Hank. It's Tony."

Hank looked at him blankly.

"Tony Falco. Remember?"

The man's breathing was laboured. Hank continued to stare.

"Tony Falco. Hank, you and I go way back, remember? Let me in, please. I gotta talk to you."

Falco? Falco? Hank said the name over and over in his head. Suddenly the penny dropped.

Tony Falco. He and Hank sure *did* go back a long way. Hank had arrested him a million times in the past; back in the 1950s, when he'd been the LAPD's Captain Kane. But what on earth was Falco doing here, in twenty-first century Scotland? And why was he so keen to speak to Hank?

Hank pulled the window open wide and told the man to come in. Falco stumbled in through the open window and fell onto the sofa, opposite Hank's desk.

"Thanks, Hank. I appreciate you letting me in. You have *no idea* how much trouble I had finding you. What are you doing in Glasgow?"

Hank sighed. "It's a long story, Tony. Why don't you tell me why *you're* here first? Then maybe we'll get round to me."

Falco nodded. "Maybe you'd better take a seat, Hank. We could be in for a long night."

As Hank looked at Tony carefully, he noticed that he seemed to almost shimmer. He looked like some sort of hologram that was flickering on and off. It was as if he was coming and going.

Hank pulled up his office chair in front of

Falco. As he listened to him talking, more and more facts about the man came back to him.

Falco was a small time cat burglar whom Hank had caught and imprisoned on more than one occasion. However, each time Falco was released he went straight back to his old ways and it was never long before he re-offended.

He'd never really hit the big time, always picking on easy targets such as small businesses or jewellery shops. These were easy to check out in terms of alarm systems, closing times and bank deposit times.

Falco's weakness however, was that he wasn't exactly the brightest diamond in the swag-bag and so usually left clues behind him which any detective worth their salt could pick up on. And Hank Kane had been worth his salt.

Hank brought his mind back to the present and listened to Falco's story.

"As you know, Hank, my family is of Italian ancestry. What you probably didn't know is that a branch of the family settled in Glasgow in the 1920s. They became, as many Italians in Scotland did, ice-cream tycoons."

Hank had come to learn that Glasgow was full

of Italians. Ice- cream parlours, restaurants, fish and chip shops; the Italians had the food scene all wrapped up. So Falco's people had been pasta pioneers in Glasgow, thought Hank. Who'd have thought it?

"*You'd* made sure I could never work in LA," continued Falco, "or probably anywhere in the States. I tried so hard to cover my tracks, to get you off my trail..."

"The only thing that nearly got me off your trail was the number of clues you left everywhere!" said Hank laughing. " You really weren't cut out for the international jewel thief business."

"Okay, so eventually, I wised up to that. My father's brother offered to help me go straight; give up crime altogether. I liked the idea of a fresh start, so I joined the ice-cream empire my uncle had founded. Don't ask my why ice-cream sold so well in this rain-soaked city, but it did."

"But..." ventured Hank.

"Well, you've guessed what the 'but' is Hank. Me? Go straight? I was kidding myself. I looked around this town and couldn't believe how few security precautions storeowners took, particularly jewellery storeowners! I know all that's changed now. But back then, it was just too easy. But, my uncle still thought I'd gone straight and the pressure of letting him down, after all he'd done for me….it lead me to plan just one…"

"…last job," finished Hank. He'd heard the "One Last Job" sob story a million times.

So, Falco explained, this time he'd targeted one of the larger jewellery stores in downtown Glasgow, setting his sights just a little higher this time. He planned the job as meticulously as his limited brain would allow and amazingly, everything had gone according to plan. Everything that is, until the owner's son arrived at the shop in the early hours of the morning, contrary to the pattern which had been set in the past.

Falco had worked out that he had five hours in which to carry out the robbery but here was the owner's son turning up just a couple of hours into the job. Falco panicked, stuffed what jewellery he had managed to take into a suitcase and tried to flee. Trouble was he tripped and fell, knocking over a display cabinet which smashed and set off the one alarm he'd forgotten to turn off.

He ran out of the shop and down a lane, hotly pursued by the son. In his haste he didn't see a dustcart reversing into the lane. Hank could imagine the panic Falco must have felt when he knew he was facing certain death.

Tony had tried to find a way around the cart but had realised that he was trapped. He'd screamed out to the driver to stop but the driver wasn't able to hear him above the sounds of rubbish being crushed inside the cart.

Tony had pushed himself back against the wall, trying to shrink, trying to make his body disappear. He had hoped against hope that the cart would somehow stop but of course it didn't and he'd been crushed to death.

Hank peered more closely at Falco and could see the marks on his ghostly arms and torso where the dustcart had pinned him to the wall, before finally taking the last breath from his body. So Falco was dead, too.

"So, what do you want from me?" asked Hank.

"I need your help, Hank," pleaded Falco.

"Look, I know we haven't exactly been good friends in the past."

Hank smirked and nodded in agreement.

"I always knew you were the best detective in town. Just after I died, a spooky ghoul claiming to be the Grim Reaper, just confirmed that you're still the best – even though you're dead! So, you're the only person I can think of who can get me out of this mess…"

"Which is?" questioned Hank.

"Which is," continued Falco, "that I've been before the Court of Ghouls – you've met those guys, haven't you?"

Hank nodded. "Unfortunately. Go on…"

"Yeah, exactly. So you'll know that they're not the most understanding of dudes. And they won't allow me to cross over into 'Bandit Heaven' until I hand over the jewels."

Hank knew what Tony meant by the term, "Bandit Heaven". He was learning more and more about the people TG called, "the in-betweens". These were people like Hank and Tony who were dead, but whose souls were being kept in a murky twilight world between being alive and being totally dead.

These "in-betweens" all had their own vision of heaven. In Hank's case, it was "Detective Heaven" – a wonderful place where all cases were solved easily. That was why Hank played ball with the Court Of Ghouls.

So "Bandit Heaven" was where burglars like Tony Falco could steal the most dazzling diamonds all day long without getting caught.

Hank sighed. "Look, Tony, the jewels are of no use to you now. Why don't you just hand them over?"

"I don't have them, Hank! That's just it. I don't have the jewels or I *would* hand them back."

Hank shook his head and stood up. "I'm tired, Tony, I really don't have time for this. You and I played enough of these cat and mouse games in the past but I'm just not up to it anymore. You can find your own way out. Use the door this time, if you don't mind. I'm off to bed."

"But Hank," protested Falco, his voice becoming louder. "I really don't have the jewels. I only wish I did. I'm tired, like you must be Hank, of wandering this 'never-never land', belonging nowhere. All I want in the world right now is to be able to put my head down and rest but I can't until I hand over the jewels!

Don't you see, Hank, someone must have been following me that night. When I was killed, they stole the jewels. Someone knew what I was up to that night, and decided they wanted a piece of the action. I don't even know where my remains are, Hank, I haven't even had a proper burial. Please Hank, don't turn your back on me. I wouldn't come to you if I could think of another way round this. You're my last hope."

Hank looked carefully at Falco. Maybe, just maybe, he was telling the truth, for once in his life. What reason would he have to lie? Stupid he may be, but even *he* must realise that jewels were of no use to a dead guy. But then, where was his body? Where were the jewels?

"Okay, Tony, I'll give you the benefit of the doubt just this once. What do you need me to do?"

They were interrupted by the door of the office squeaking. Falco turned around. There was no mistaking the smell of rotting flesh which floated through the air as the tall, black cloaked figure entered the room. Falco flinched. No horror could compare to the *thing* that had just entered the room!

Carrying his scythe in one bloodied hand, the thing's face was ghostly white, made worse by the eerie light which partially lit the room. His black cloak covered him from head to toe, the hood draped loosely around his face. Red coals burned where there should have been eyes and his rotting teeth completed his skull-like appearance. The Grim Reaper pulled up a chair and sat down.

"Hey, TG," said Hank. "I understand you guys have already met. Very kind of you to offer to help Falco find the jewels." A note of suspicion was in his voice.

"Just call me 'public spirited', Hank," said the Grim Reaper winking.

CHAPTER TWO

ANNIE MAKES HER ESCAPE

ANNIE pushed her hair back from her face. She was hot and sweaty after the tiring game of volleyball she'd just played. She looked around wondering what game was going to be played next. Unfortunately for her, all the outdoor sports were over. The youth club were now concentrating on what Annie called "girlie things".

Annie (or "Ace", as her brother Charlie liked to call her in order to make her sound more like a detective) hated all "girlie things". Her hair was long but only because her mother insisted on her keeping it that way. Annie always wore it tied back from her face, any tendrils which escaped being hastily pushed back out of her way.

She *never* wore dresses, much to her mother's dismay, preferring instead to pull on her denims and football shirt, even when she attended one of the many parties she was invited to.

She didn't particularly enjoy the parties, nor understand quite why she was invited. She never joined in with party games such as "pass the parcel", preferring instead to join the boys outside in the garden for a game of football. She was always asked to join both teams, each captain disappointed when they didn't get her on their side.

It was holiday time and yet again, Annie's mother had insisted she attend the local youth club. Annie's protests that she'd be okay on her own fell on deaf ears. Her mother didn't trust Charlie to take care of his sister either! And this was without knowing the full extent of her children's previous adventures with the Dead Detective.

She knew of course that something had happened but she believed that it was the police that had solved everything. All her children had done was talk about the cases with Hank round at his office, while drinking coke and eating hamburgers no doubt.

Just as well she never knew that Charlie had once shared a freezer with a chopped up body and that he and Annie had had to run for their lives! No, that definitely would have been too much information for Mrs Christian.

Annie took a drink from the cold can of Coke she had just got from the machine and looked around her. Face painting. Hair braiding. How to decorate your fingernails. She sighed heavily. She was bored. She wondered what Charlie was doing. Certainly not braiding anybody's hair.

She put the Coke can on a nearby table and made her way to the exit. "Just going to the toilet," she shouted when one of the club leaders looked in her direction.

With a bit of luck, she'd be so distracted by braiding hair that she'd never notice when Annie didn't return

CHAPTER THREE

CHARLIE ON THE CASE

CHARLIE, on the other hand, was having a ball. He was in a music store on one of Glasgow's High Streets. Almost all of his pocket money was spent on buying CDs and each one was carefully placed in alphabetical order in the huge CD holder he had at home. He knew, instantly, if Annie had put her mucky paws on them and boy did she pay a high price!

He examined the CD he'd been hankering after since last Saturday. He was torn between that and a brilliant video he'd seen. The CD won. He paid for it at the desk and left the store, happily clutching the new addition to his collection.

It was a beautiful, sunny day and Charlie hummed as he walked. He was still a little early. Hank had asked him call in, saying that this case needed at least one living detective!

Arriving at Hank's office in Gordon Street, Charlie pushed open the downstairs entrance door and ran up the first flight of stairs. He arrived at the second floor and knew, instantly that TG was home. There was just no mistaking that all too familiar stench.

When Charlie had first met Hank, he'd been looking for an assistant and up until the last case Charlie had been kept in the dark about most things. However, when Hank's hand had been forced, Charlie had learnt all about the Dead Detective.

The first time he'd visited Hank's office he'd been amazed by the décor but now he was used to it. The last time Charlie had seen a huge black telephone like Hank's had been in a Humphrey Bogart movie!

Charlie pushed open the door of Hank's office and was forced to take a step backwards. He'd expected to find Hank and TG but now there was a third dead body. Now that was just a bit *too* much!

To Hank and TG, who were well used to the sight of dead bodies, Falco hadn't appeared particularly gross. To Charlie, however, Falco's appearance was shocking. His flickering shape of a body looked crushed and bloodied from his terrible death. The upper part of his torso was completely caved in and both arms were broken in more than one place from where he had tried to shield his body.

His facial features, even when he spoke, remained frozen in a grotesque mask of horror, exactly the way he had looked when he died. Charlie shivered, tried to compose himself, and pulled up a seat beside Hank.

Hank made the introductions. Tony Falco offered the vague shape of his hand for Charlie to shake. Charlie took a cup of cold water from the cooler, smiled briefly at the newcomer and pretended not to see Falco's extended hand. Each time he thought things couldn't get much weirder he was proven wrong. He took a sip of water and sat back to listen. This had to be worth hearing!

CHAPTER FOUR

IN BUSINESS AGAIN

FALCO went off to float around Glasgow, leaving the two detectives to discuss the story they'd just heard. TG had gone to bed, exhausted by the hectic social life he led.

Hank was unsure of the benefit of taking on the case, though he had to admit he was interested in it. Charlie was interested in *everything* he heard these days, unable to resist the possibility of being involved in solving a mystery. He leaned forward in his chair, excited at the prospect of being in on a new case.

"Where exactly in Scotland did the crime take place?" he asked anxiously.

"In this dear, green place, as you Glaswegians fondly like to call it," replied Hank. "In one of the larger shops in the Argyle Arcade. I'll show you which one if I decide to take on the case."

"What do you mean, 'if you decide'?" spluttered Charlie. "You have to take the case. It's another chance for you to cross over to 'Detective Heaven' – a chance for me to practise my skills; a chance..." and he knew he was clutching at straws, "... to help Falco be finally laid to rest."

Hank raised an eyebrow at this last remark. Like, he cared. He did, however, think over the kid's other remarks.

Charlie had a point. So long as Hank refused to take on cases, there was no progress to be made in getting over to the other side. And sometimes he was tired. Tired of the continual grind, tired of each day being the same as the one before. Tired of having nowhere to lay his weary head, where he would never again awaken.

He reached for yet another sip of his chemical compound, the one that kept the flesh on his weary bones and nodded his acceptance.

"Okay, Kid, we're on."

CHAPTER FIVE

INVADER

CHARLIE went into his bedroom and knew, instantly, that someone had been there. Something, he didn't quite know what, was out of place. He closed the door gently behind him and put the CD on his bed. Two-thirty in the afternoon. Mum wouldn't have been home, she was still at work, and his sister, Ace, was at her youth club.

He looked around the room and then he spotted it. One of his CD cases was lying on the floor. He *never* left cases on the floor. He was meticulous about his music, each CD was kept in its proper case and put on the CD rack in alphabetical order. Always.

He lifted the case. He hadn't played this particular piece of music for a long time. But he *did* know someone who liked it.

He flung open his cupboard doors and pulled his sister out by the arm.

"What are you doing here, Ace? You're not meant to be here. And how many times have I told you to keep out of my room?"

Annie shook herself free and opened her mouth to protest.

"How did you even get in here? Mum didn't give you a key. She wouldn't have trusted you to be in the house alone. Anyway, you should be at the youth club. And how dare you touch my CDs…"

"IF you'd just give me a chance to speak," shouted Annie indignantly, "I'll try to explain."

Charlie sat down on the bed and folded his arms. "Okay, shoot."

Annie took a deep breath. "I know you won't understand, Charlie, in fact I don't expect you to understand, but you have no idea, honestly, how boring the youth club is. All they're interested in is prettying you up, teaching you how to use make-up, how to make your hair nice. Yuck! I'm just not interested."

Charlie tried to hide a grin. Looking at Annie standing in front of him, clothed in denims and trainers; he could understand her reluctance to take part in anything so girlish.

"Go on," he looked at his sister.

"Well, that's it, really. I'm not interested, Charlie, I'd rather be at home."

He raised an eyebrow, trying to imitate Hank.

"*You* know what I mean, " she continued. "You don't have to spend your time with stupid girls who can't play football. They can't even understand the offside rule!" she exclaimed indignantly, sitting down on the bed beside him.

"Look, Charlie, I know I said before that detective work is boring but that was before I went to this youth club! Next to that place, detective stuff is positively exciting! Please don't tell Mum, Charlie, please. You know how angry she'll be."

Annie's sixth sense had told her that Charlie was on a case. All the signs were there. He had a buzz about him and he was almost bearable to live with, which was definitely not a normal state of affairs. And although she didn't want to admit it, she had been fascinated when Charlie had told her the whole story behind the Dead Detective.

Charlie sighed. "Even if I don't tell her, Ace, someone from the club will. You're their responsibility while you're at the club, and they can't just have kids disappearing off home without letting anyone know."

Annie nodded. "'Spose so," she said, looking downcast. "What am I going to do?"

Anger gone, Charlie began to relent. "Okay, I'll make a deal with you. But you *have* to keep to your side of the bargain."

Annie looked at him expectantly.

"I'll take you back to the youth club now…"

Annie began to protest but Charlie put up his hand to silence her.

"I'll take you back to the youth club now," he repeated, "but you have to stay there. On condition that you do, I'll tell your leader you had to go to the dentist. I'll say that I came to pick you up but forgot to tell them."

Annie stared at the carpet.

"But I don't *want* to go back, Charlie, I want to…"

"Up to you, Ace. Either we go back now and offer an explanation, or you wait till someone tells Mum and see what she has to say about it."

Annie sighed and stood up. She really had no choice. "Okay, let's go. Better get back before I miss the cookie baking."

The two of them left the house, Charlie locking the door behind him.

"Oh, and Charlie?"

"Yes?"

"Stop calling me, Ace."

CHAPTER SIX

THE MIST

IT WAS dark and had suddenly got very cold. Charlie shivered and wished he'd worn something warmer. He rubbed his hands together for warmth and wished Hank would hurry up. He checked his watch. Ten-thirty. Where was Hank?

The two had arranged to meet at the entrance of a well-known jewellery centre in Glasgow so that they could examine the crime scene. Not that either of them thought it would be of much help; the crime having taken place some fifty years previously. It would be doubtful if they would find any traces of evidence.

At last, Charlie made out Hank's familiar figure coming towards him. Hank's unfortunate habit of shedding flesh during daylight hours meant that it was easier for the two to work in the evenings, hence Charlie's frequent late night forays into Glasgow.

Hank smiled a greeting at Charlie and the two made their way towards the largest jewellers on the corner. It was a family owned business and the sign outside read:

Hatcliff
Est. 1932

"They've been here for round about seventy years," remarked Hank. "So this place was definitely here fifty years ago when Falco carried out the botched robbery. Wonder if there's anything to be gained by trying to get inside."

Himself and Charlie went to the back of the shop and checked out the doors. Everything was firmly bolted, the doors and windows were barred and there was an alarm system in operation. They left and walked in the direction Falco would have taken all those years ago; towards the nearby alleyway. The place where he had lost his life.

Charlie walked on ahead, Hank following at a slower pace, his eyes taking in every part of the alley. A light mist was starting to come down, lowering the temperature even further. Glasgow summers! Hank would never become accustomed to them. He often joked that you

could tell when it was summer in Scotland –
because around June, the snow turned into rain.

As Hank had suspected, the alley contained
nothing more than any other alley did.
Overflowing rubbish bins, empty cans and
cigarette butts. He took another few paces and
spotted something shiny on the ground. A piece
of gold paper, he thought, nothing very
interesting.

However, something about the way it was
almost embedded in the ground made him
stoop down to pick it up. He was amazed to find
that it was a small and very delicate gold earring.
He fingered it thoughtfully and looked around
to see if he could find the other one. Nothing.
Hank looked doubtfully at the earring. Either
lady luck had thrown him a rare smile, or
someone else had planted this earring here.
Time for a second opinion, he thought.

"Charlie," he shouted, "come see what I've
found."

Silence.

He shouted more loudly this time. The last
time he'd seen Charlie he'd been making his
way towards the far end of the alley. Hank

turned to walk in the same direction, quickening his pace.

Again, he shouted Charlie's name. Again, silence.

Hank reached the end of the alley and stood on what was probably the same spot where Tony Falco had been killed all those years ago. He stopped and looked around.

Except for Hank and the gold earring, the alley was completely empty.

CHAPTER SEVEN
ACE FOR HIRE

DAWN was almost breaking by the time Hank returned to his office. He was reluctant to return home at all but he had no choice as the first sign of daylight meant the flesh would start falling from his bones. He sank wearily into his chair and drank deeply from the bottle that contained his flesh-restoring chemical compound.

Where on earth was Charlie? Hank couldn't understand it. The kid had simply disappeared. He had retraced his steps a million times but was still no closer to finding the kid. It was as though he never existed, as though he had the ability to walk through walls and disappear into thin air.

Hank shook his head. He was worried, confused and tired. What should he do next? Charlie was just a kid, though he liked to think he was a lot more grown up. Hank always felt responsible for him, especially when they were working on cases which required them to work in the dead of night.

He didn't know he had fallen asleep until he was awakened by a light tapping on the office door. He pushed his hat back on his head and shouted: "Come in."

Annie entered the office.

"Hi, Hank," she said, rather shyly. "I'm sorry to trouble you and I hope that Charlie explained…"

Hank looked at her expectantly.

"It's just that he said I could help out around the office for the next few days," she explained. However, she couldn't help adding, "I don't want to go back to the youth club and he said this would keep me out of mischief."

Hank frowned.

"He, *did* tell you, didn't he?" asked Annie, looking doubtfully at the detective. "I mean, I don't want to butt in where I'm not wanted but Charlie told me a bit about the case and it sounds soooo exciting… and I'd just love to help. I promise I won't get in your way, Hank, honest I won't. I'll be ever so quiet, and stay in the background, and just help out when you want me to…"

Hank held up his hand to silence her. He

couldn't help but be amused. He *had* hoped that Annie was about to tell him where her brother was, not to tell him she had come to work for him! Not that he minded, an extra pair of hands was always welcome but now he had to tell her that he had "lost" her brother.

He forced a smile. "Sit down Annie, or should I call you Ace?"

Annie sat down and took one of the chocolate biscuits Hank offered. "I suppose 'Ace' will do. Charlie always calls me that. I suppose I should try and get used to it."

She bit hungrily into the biscuit. She had left home in such a rush this morning she'd had no time for breakfast and now found she was starving. She hoped Hank would offer her another.

Hank cleared his throat. He had no idea where to begin.

"Charlie and I started work on the case last night. We went to the scene of the crime and had a quick look around."

Annie nodded. "And were you able to find anything?" she asked.

Hank was grateful for the diversion. He

wanted to put off telling her about her brother for as long as he possibly could!

"I *did* find something, now that you ask," he replied, reaching into his pocket. He pulled out the earring and placed it on the desk between himself and Annie. She reached out to touch it, then noticed that her fingers were covered in chocolate and thought better of it. She licked most of the chocolate off her fingers and picked up the earring.

"Very nice," she said, trying to sound like an expert. "But is it connected to the case in any way? I mean, what are the chances of an earring that might have been dropped fifty years ago still being in the same spot, Mr Kane?"

Hank nodded. "That's what we have to find out." He tapped the side of his nose. "Looks like you and me got some detecting to do, huh?"

"Okay," she nodded, taking immediately to the task. "Did Charlie spend last night here with you? I don't think he came home or, if he did, he left really early this morning."

"No," replied Hank, "he didn't spend the night here." He hesitated. "Have another biscuit," he said, offering Annie the plate, as he prepared to tell her about the events of the night before.

Annie was deeply shocked.

"Let's call the cops!" she exclaimed

"Dead guys can't call the cops," said Hank.

"What will I tell my mum?"

"I'm confident I'll solve this, Annie. You gotta trust me, OK? Tell your mother that Charlie's working on a case here with me. She seems to think I know what I'm doing. Not sure that would still be true if we told her that her son had disappeared! Trust me, give me a few days."

Annie thought about it. She thought about their last case together. She decided to trust Hank's detecting skills.

"OK," she said.

"This one's up to us, Ace."

CHAPTER EIGHT
GOLDEN CLUE

HANK re-read the case notes he had managed to get from TG. No-one had ever been caught for the robbery and the stolen jewels had never been found. The jeweller's son, Guy Hatcliff, said that he had chased the robber up an alleyway but lost sight of him. No dustcart was ever mentioned. So either Falco was lying, or Hatcliff was. Either way, Hank had to move, and move fast. His young assistant was missing, and Hank felt entirely responsible.

Annie had taken the gold earring to a contact of TG's to be valued. She would have to be Hank's eyes and ears during the daylight hours, just as Charlie had been.

Annie returned, flushed with excitement at the thrill of being entrusted with such a precious item. She had carried it in a small black box lined with cotton wool ever so carefully both to and from the shop. She had stood over the man while he looked at the jewellery through his eyepiece. He had examined it gently, giving the jewellery the respect it deserved. Annie had looked on with pride. This was *her* adventure and it was already a lot more exciting than the youth club!

The man had given her a valuation on a piece of headed paper which she'd folded in half then in half again and placed inside her pocket. All the way home she checked every now and again to make sure both the paper and the box were where they should have been.

She placed both items on the desk in front of Hank. "There you go, Hank. I told you I wouldn't be long, now didn't I?"

Hank smiled and unfolded the piece of paper. The heading on the paper read:

> Hetherington & Sons
> Valuers since 1902

and underneath was written:

> Gold earring: 1 only
> Value (single)
>
> £ 35,000
>
> Value (as part of pair)   £ 129,000

The man had then added:

> These earrings date back to
> Victorian times. They are incredibly
> ornate and cut as of that time.
> Doubtful if the shop in question
> would stock these now, more likely
> to find them in an antique jewellers.

Hank opened the box and took out the earring again. "But what was it doing lying in the middle of the alley in the year 2003?" he said almost to himself.

Annie wondered if Charlie would have been able to give Hank an answer. For her part, she had no idea, so she decided to keep quiet.

TG came into the room. Annie had heard all about the Grim Reaper from Charlie. She was unfazed by his appearance, having been more freaked out by some of the fashion she saw every day at school! Hank smiled to himself.

TG pulled up a chair and nodded towards Annie. Hank looked at him thoughtfully.

"Any more thoughts on this case, TG?" he asked of the Reaper.

"May do," replied TG, wiping the sleep from his bleary eyes. "What do you need to know?"

Hank laughed. "Are you kidding? We know almost nothing. Any information would be helpful, TG."

"Aw Hank, gimme a break, man. You know I'm not supposed to help you. You'll only get yourself into trouble again."

Hank sighed. TG was right. He and Annie would have to go this one alone. Trouble was, he had no idea where to go from here! He was stumped. This was rare. Rarer still, he was close to admitting it to himself.

"By the way, Hank. I've got something for you. Here, take this." TG passed Hank a small bottle, a hip flask in fact.

"What on earth is this? Another potion? What am I? A wizard or something? I got enough weird drinks, TG…"

"But you'll need this Hank. Looks like your gonna have to be out and about during daylight if you're gonna solve this case. And your other potion only works at night. We gotta make sure you're presentable, Hank – at least, as presentable as your ugly self can be! Ha ha! TG paused, and waited in vain for the others to join in the laughter. "What's the matter with you both? I'm a funny guy, really."

TG pulled himself stiffly up from his chair and groaned.

"Anyway, Hank. Take this stuff and use it *very* sparingly. It's expensive… I mean, *strong* stuff. So swig it whenever your skin starts to fall off. Otherwise, you might get some funny looks!"

"As many as you, TG?" snapped Hank, reluctantly putting the hip flask in his pocket.

"How do you put up with Hank's sarcasm, kid?" asked TG, looking at Annie.

"Charlie is the 'Kid'. I'm Ace, if you *have* to insist on a nickname," answered Annie.

"Hmmph," mumbled TG, "looks like you guys will get on just fine. Think I'll get me some coffee. Helps me think." TG turned to Hank and said: "Ever tried that new twenty-four hour coffee shop in Barr Street, Hank?"

Hank shook his head.

"Should try it, it's a helluva bean they brew down there, Hank. It's just the other side of the alleyway you were talking about. Actually, I have some deals of my own brewing somewhere else. You guys go on, maybe I'll catch you up." And with that, he left the room.

Annie noticed that TG had left a note pad on the chair he'd been sitting on. It looked like a reporter's small notebook. She picked it up and went to follow him but Hank stopped her.

"Lemme see that, Ace."

Annie looked surprised but when she saw Hank's face as he leafed through TG's notebook, she realised that it contained very interesting information.

"I'd better keep this safe," he said.

"Keep it safe for TG?" asked Annie

"Yeah, something like that," replied Hank putting it in his pocket.

Annie suddenly understood that TG leaving his notebook behind was no accident. However, she knew that's exactly the story both he and Hank would stick to should they ever be asked. She just hoped *she* wouldn't be asked! She turned to Hank.

"I think TG means for us to go to the coffee shop, Mr Kane. Some sort of clue there, maybe?" she said.

"Maybe," smiled Hank.

He took his hat from its stand at the door and checked his watch. After seven o'clock. He took a swig from his chemical compound and opened the office door. He should be able to keep his flesh on, for the moment.

He closed the door behind him as he and Annie left the building.

CHAPTER NINE

COFFEE WITH KIERAN

HANK and Annie sat in the quietest corner of the coffee shop. The place was busy. Word had obviously got around that the coffee was good and every table was pretty much full. Annie blew bubbles into her milk shake through her straw then, realising she must look childish in Hank's eyes, immediately stopped and began to sip the milk shake directly from the glass.

Hank hadn't noticed; he was too busy observing the customers. There was something very familiar about the guy who was sitting on a high bar stool reading his newspaper. Or *pretending* to read his newspaper. To Hank's trained eye, it was pretty obvious the guy was only skimming the pages. Instead of reading, he was listening to the hum of conversation that was going on around him.

Now Hank realised why TG had suggested that himself and Annie come here. It was another little bit of... not exactly help... but a guide in the right direction. Hank hoped the Court Of Ghouls would see it that way!

Hank kept looking at the man. He looked like he was about seventy, well dressed and smartly groomed. Hank never forgot a face, and he knew if he stared for long enough he'd remember who the guy was.

Suddenly it came to him! He'd seen his picture in the newspaper recently. That's the guy, thought Hank, who'd single-handedly caught two robbers in the act of robbing a jewellery store in the West End?

The thieves appeared to have thrown the jewels into the River Kelvin as they were tackled by the man Hank was now observing. The jewels were never recovered, and of course, the thieves tried to say that they'd been caught before they'd had a chance to steal anything. But who would believe two thieves, with a track record that the courts knew well?

Hank nudged Annie to follow him and the two walked over to where the man was sitting. Hank offered his hand.

"Hank Kane," he drawled in his American accent. "Hope you don't mind me interrupting but I've seen your picture in the newspaper. You really surprised those guys huh?"

The man looked back at him with more than a hint of suspicion in his eyes. "Kieran Smith," he said, taking Hank's hand and shaking it weakly.

"And this here's my... err... niece, Annie."

"Hi Mr Smith, nice to meet you. It's not every day I meet a local hero."

She too had recognised him.

Hank soon had Kieran engaged in conversation. He was practised in the art of fooling people, pretending to be someone other than he was.

He found it easy to lie to Kieran, telling him he was in Scotland to visit his sister, Annie's mother, and would be returning to the States in the next month or so.

Kieran Smith relaxed a little. He was getting used to complete strangers introducing themselves. After all, he was something of a celebrity now.

But, while Hank's conversation seemed perfectly innocent, he knew certain things about Kieran Smith. For instance, he already knew that

Kieran's father and the mother of Guy Hatcliff (the guy from the from the jewellery store) were cousins. It had all been in TG's notes.

Hank also knew that there'd been a huge family feud fifty years ago and that Kieran Smith's relations had ended up being on the poor side of the family, shut out by their richer relations.

There was much rivalry and bitterness and neither side had mentioned the others' names for years. What Hank didn't know yet was the cause of the feud.

But things had changed recently. Josh Smith and Lydia Hatcliff, the latest generation of the feuding families, had changed the way the families thought about each other. Josh and Lydia had met by chance at a dinner party, began dating and soon became engaged.

Though initially the engagement had been met with some anger, both families realised that they had no choice but to accept the impending wedding and so, reluctantly, the feud was put to rest.

Hank knew, therefore, that if he could get on the right side of Kieran Smith, it would open

up doors to the world of Hatcliff, the jewellers.
Then Hank would get closer to solving the case
of the disappearing jewellery. And, the case of
his disappearing assistant.

CHAPTER TEN

THE BELLS ARE RINGING...

HANK knew something very spooky was going on and his instincts were beginning to kick in. "We gotta get an invite to the wedding or at least to the reception," he said, back at the office.

Annie looked at him, somewhat doubtfully. "And just how do you think you're going to manage that, Hank? I take it you mean the Smith and Hatcliff wedding? It'll be one of the biggest weddings Glasgow has seen for years. And you think you can get an invite? Get real."

Hank started pacing up and down the office but then began to smile. "I'll get an invite, and one for you, too."

Annie shrugged but kept her mouth shut. She'd said quite enough for the time being. Besides, if Hank was happy to believe he could go up to a guy in a coffee shop, speak to him once, then get an invite to his relative's wedding, well then, who was she to argue?

*　　　*　　　*　　　*　　　*　　　*　　　*

When Annie arrived in Hank's office the next day, she couldn't believe her eyes. There, on the desk in front of her, was the invitation. The wedding invitation she said Hank would never manage to obtain. A beautiful, cream-coloured card bound with peach ribbon and lettered in gold. Hank had opened it so that she could read the words inside:

*Mr & Mrs J Hatcliff have great pleasure
in requesting the company of:*

Mr Hank Kane & Miss Annie Christian

*To the wedding reception of their daughter:
Ms Lydia Hatcliff
to
Mr Joshua Smith
Saturday, 13 July 2003
2:30 pm
At the City Centre Hotel
RSVP*

"But that's tomorrow, Hank," Annie finally managed to stammer. "And just how did you get an invitation? It's a society wedding – these invites are harder to come by than tickets to the World Cup."

Hank smiled knowingly. "That's for me to know and you to find out. Let's just say that some of my 'un-dead' friends come in pretty handy at times."

The truth of the matter was that Hank had gone to the *Cesspit* Nightclub and rounded up a few of the dead guys TG hung out with. They'd obliged him by visiting the Hatcliff residence and stealing one of the invites while they were in their invisible guise. They'd brought it over to Hank so that he could change the names on the invite. Easy!

Annie sat down, dumbfounded. "I hope this doesn't mean I have to wear a dress," she said, as she picked at the pocket of her dungarees.

"Well…" said Hank, smiling. "You sure can't go looking like you do, or else we'll both be asked to leave."

Annie sighed. "Okay, I'll do it, but just this once. And I'm not doing it for you." Her voice became very low. "I'm doing it for Charlie."

Hank nodded. He was becoming increasingly

worried about the kid. He had gone back to the alleyway where Charlie had disappeared but had been unable to find further clues. He had even taken one of his ghoulish friends from the *Cesspit* with him to help him with a spot of "wall walking".

Hank had never quite managed to master the art of making your body transparent so that you were able to walk straight through walls and out the other side. The boys from the *Cesspit*, however, were experts. Despite this skill, they failed to find any magical entrances or exits or any obvious ways in which Charlie could have disappeared.

The only thing Hank had found in the alleyway was a bottle full of strange-coloured liquid. The bottle had aged and the writing had become illegible but Hank was pretty sure what the contents were.

He stood up. "Let's go," he said to Annie. "Can't sit about here moping, we've got work to do."

Annie managed a small smile and joined him. Together, the two of them left the building.

CHAPTER ELEVEN

THE MIST RETURNS

"EMBALMING fluid, Hank, you got yourself a bottle of embalming fluid," confirmed the pathologist, as he removed his glasses and recapped the lid on the bottle. Jack Russell was retired now, but he'd been a pathologist for more years than he cared to remember. And he knew his stuff.

He was one of the "mortal" contacts Hank had made in Glasgow. Hank had been a good judge of character. He'd known who to trust with his whole "I'm dead" story.

"I've seen enough of this in my lifetime to know what it is. Looks like old stock. Where'd you get it?"

"I found it in an alley in the city centre," replied Hank. "It's the alley beside Hatcliff jewellers, the place that was robbed about fifty years ago. The one where neither the jewels nor the thief were ever found."

Jack nodded. "It's not surprising you found embalming fluid there, Hank. That used to be the site of a factory where coffins were made. Embalming fluid was bottled there as well."

It all started to make sense to Hank. The eerie mist which seemed to fill the alleyway no matter what the weather was like; the sudden coldness which enveloped you when you entered and the general feeling of unrest. He wondered if it was possible that there were spirits there which had never quite been laid to rest. Evil spirits who bore grudges, perhaps over the manner of their deaths. And could they explain Charlie's disappearance?

"Thanks, Jack," said Hank, as he lifted the bottle and placed it in the pocket of his raincoat.

"Any time, Hank, you know where I am," said Jack, as he walked with them to his front door.

Hank and Annie waved goodbye and headed for the local library. They were going to check up on old records which related to the original case. They spent the day there and left the library just before dusk.

"Let's take one more look in the alleyway, Hank," pleaded Annie. "I want to see for myself where Charlie disappeared. Please, you never know, I might see something you've missed."

Hank doubted that very much but he hadn't the heart to refuse her. Besides, no harm would be done in re-visiting the alleyway and, with darkness beginning to fall, he felt more secure about his appearance.

Annie shivered as she turned the corner and arrived at the entrance of the alley.

"Told you so," said Hank. "It's colder here than any other part of the city." He shivered and pulled his raincoat more tightly around his body.

"Stay beside me, Ace, I don't want to lose you, too. That was Charlie's mistake, wandering away into the mist. Stay near and at least that means that if one of us disappears then both of us will."

Annie was quite happy to stay beside the detective. Though she wouldn't have admitted it for the world, she was scared. There was something more than just a little creepy about the place!

Hank kept to the left side of the wall, feeling the brickwork as he walked. He'd already done this a few times before, checking for loose bricks, anywhere Charlie could have gone.

Annie stopped suddenly and caught Hank's arm. "Did you hear that?" she whispered.

"Hear what?" asked Hank, he too was keeping his voice hushed.

"A voice, faint, but definitely a voice. Asking for help. Ssh! There it is again."

Hank strained his ears but could hear nothing. She was imagining things.

"I can't hear a thing, Ace." He spoke in normal tones now. "Come on, let's go a bit further..."

Annie wasn't listening. Instead she was walking ahead of him, as if in a trance, as though following someone or something. She was almost running now, her body becoming enveloped in the mist which swirled around her.

Hank quickened his pace and managed to grab her hand.

"Wait for me, Annie. Where are you going?"

She didn't answer. She just stared straight ahead and concentrated on whatever it was she could hear.

Hank was unnerved but knew he had little choice but to stay with her. A newspaper rustled as it caught around his feet and drops of rain began to fall. But Annie kept on walking, her eyes never wavering from whatever focal point she was concentrating on straight ahead.

They reached what seemed to be the end of the alleyway, only this time there was a corner to be turned.

Hank knew the alleyway had been a dead end before – there hadn't been a corner. He was pretty sure of that.

Annie stopped abruptly and Hank heard her sharp intake of breath as the mist suddenly cleared and they could see what lay before them.

A large, wooden coffin lay on the ground, its lid covered in dust and leaves. Hank could hear the voice now. It came from inside the wooden box.

"Help me, Ace! You've got to help me. I'm suffocating in here! I can't breathe. Get me out!"

It was Charlie's voice! Hank couldn't believe it. Charlie was here! They had found him!

The coffin lid wasn't screwed down, indeed it lay slightly askew as though someone had tried to open it, or indeed push it off.

Annie brushed forward past Hank and knelt beside the coffin.

"I'm here, Charlie," she cried. "Don't worry, I'll get you out."

She tried to push the lid of the coffin but it was far too heavy. Hank knelt down beside her and began to push as well. Finally the lid fell to the ground and there he was! Charlie!

Annie threw her arms around her brother. "Charlie, I'm so glad to see you, are you okay?" She was laughing and crying at the same time.

But the person she was hugging suddenly began to feel strange. He was no longer warm. He didn't feel the same. He didn't even smell the same. He felt cold now and as Annie pulled back slightly to look at her brother, she saw his body crumble into ashes. She screamed and jumped backwards away from the coffin.

Hank glanced from her to the box and flinched. What had looked like Charlie's human form had now begun to disintegrate and crumble. His face was grotesque, the eyes disappearing first, leaving huge gaping holes in his face. Bit by bit his whole face caved in. Then his body, and finally the coffin, too, disappeared.

It was too much for Annie and she collapsed on the floor. Hank picked her up and carried her away from her brother's remains as fast as his own disintegrating body would let him.

CHAPTER TWELVE

UP THE AISLE...

HANK made sure he took Annie straight home. He left her at the door of her house, promising that tomorrow they *would* find Charlie. The *real* Charlie.

Annie tried to smile as she said goodbye to Hank, her tear-stained face turned away quickly to hide how she really felt.

Hank made his way back to the office, now more determined than ever. He *had* to find Charlie and he *had* to solve this case.

He didn't sleep well that night, dreaming of coffins and embalming fluid and ghosts who could disappear through walls. When he finally slept soundly, he was awakened almost immediately by the Grim Reaper returning from one of his many late night clubbing sessions. Hank sighed, punched his pillow and wished TG would grow up!

Hank got up and dressed carefully, taking more care over his appearance than usual in view of the day's impending wedding.

Annie arrived at twelve o'clock, as they had arranged, looking very uncomfortable in a green dress with matching hair slides. Hank said nothing – he didn't want to make her feel any worse. He knew she'd much rather be dressed in denims and trainers!

They arrived at the church just slightly ahead of the bride. They slipped into a seat at the back and tried to look inconspicuous. Annie couldn't believe the huge puffball dress the bride was wearing and vowed there and then she'd *never* wear anything so ridiculous!

Meanwhile, Hank was thinking the same about quite a few of the guests. Most of the females wore hats, each trying to wear one bigger than the next; each wearing more ornate and vulgar jewellery than the other.

Hank spotted Kieran Smith on the left hand side of the church. He had smiled at Hank when he and Annie arrived, recognising them from their conversation in the coffee shop, then looked at them quizzically as though wondering why they were invited to this particular wedding.

Hank decided to keep out of his way for a little

while, at least until he had made up a suitable lie to tell him!

The ceremony ended and the guests made their way through the little churchyard to the waiting cars. They were soon on their way to the *City Centre Hotel* where the reception was to be held. When they arrived, Hank took the opportunity to visit the gents' toilet to drink some of his medical compound. It would never do to start losing flesh at a society wedding!

Guests were mingling but Hank and Annie remained as onlookers for the time being. Gradually someone drifted over and introduced himself.

"Jeremy Hatcliff, father of the bride. How are you?"

Hank shook his hand.

"Hank Kane, and this is my niece, Annie. Great wedding, Mr Hatcliff. We're having a lovely time."

"Glad to hear it!" boomed Jeremy. He was not renowned for his soft tones.

"Gladys, come on over here," he shouted to his wife. "Come and meet some of our guests."

Mrs Hatcliff scurried over. She was a tiny little

woman, with a tiny little voice to match. She looked as though she would faint if someone even dared to say, "boo". Hank had a terrible urge to do so, but bit his lip instead.

"Welcome," she said, bobbing up and down while her husband made the introductions. "So very nice to meet you both." She was so small, she was only the same height as Annie.

"It's lovely to meet you, Mrs Hatcliff. You have a very beautiful daughter, you must be very proud," said Hank.

Mrs Hatcliff beamed. Lydia was the light of her life. "Why thank you, yes, she *is* very beautiful, isn't she?"

Annie wished Hank would stop staring so intently at Mrs Hatcliff. Didn't he know it was bad manners? Suddenly she realised just why he was staring.

"I hope you don't mind me asking, ma'am," said Hank, stooping down to Mrs Hatcliff's level. "But I can't help admiring your earrings. Could I ask where you bought them? I'm looking for something nice to take back to my wife in the States when I return next month."

"You won't be taking these, young man,"

boomed Jeremy Hatcliff. "Or at least you won't be taking the originals." He laughed.

Hank looked at him, interested in what the man had to say.

"These are replicas," he said, pointing at the earrings.

Mrs Hatcliff touched her hair self-consciously. Sometimes she wished Jeremy wasn't quite so loud. Everybody was looking. Now everybody would know her earrings were fake. Oh dear.

"The originals disappeared years ago. Ever hear about... No, I don't suppose you would, you not coming from these parts and all. A robbery took place in our family shop some years back. The earrings were part of the haul the thief escaped with and they were never recovered. We suspected an employee of making off with them. Very nasty, complicated business."

"How come?" asked Hank, sensing Mr Hatcliff was a talkative sort when encouraged, or even when not encouraged.

"The employee was also a relative, I'm afraid. A cousin we employed when his family hit on hard times. He was just a boy at the time, 18 or

19. But we thought it was so ungrateful of him to steal from us, after all, we were only employing him out of pity. So we sacked him. Ironic then, Mr Kane, that he's here today."

"Really?" asked Annie.

"We've all to forgive and forget now of course, otherwise, my daughter would do her nut. And of course, nothing was ever proven. So… there he is there in fact," said Mr Hatcliffe, pointing at Kieran Smith!

"I admire the way you have put the past behind you, sir. You're a credit to your family. Jewels really are precious, aint they?" said Hank.

"Luckily," said Mr Hatcliffe, "my grandfather still had the original drawings for the earrings and was able to design the ones Gladys is wearing. But they're not the real thing, you understand." He drew on the large cigar he was holding, almost completely hiding Gladys behind a cloud of smoke as he did so.

Hank nodded.

"So, if nothing was ever proven, then you could say that the thief was never caught?" he asked.

Jeremy Hatcliff shook his head. "He never was,

my friend. Strangest thing. My father, Guy, gave chase to the robber but he just disappeared up an alleyway. Simply disappeared into thin air, along with the jewels! Neither thief nor jewels were ever found, though the police searched the area thoroughly on more than one occasion. Bit like the Bermuda Triangle, eh?" He slapped Hank heartily on the back.

"Yes, sure seems strange," Hank agreed.

Gladys Hatcliff was tugging on her husband's sleeve.

"Jeremy," she whispered in her squeaky little voice. "Lady Grey is over there, we really should go and speak to her." She didn't share her husband's passion for telling complete strangers her family's darkest secrets.

"What?" blustered Jeremy. "Oh right, okay, sorry to leave you Mr Kane, Miss ... sorry, what did you say your name was?"

"Annie."

"Annie. Right. Well, speak to you later. And, sorry, who did you say invited you?"

"Timothy. You know, Timothy who has the wife with the freckles on the bridge of her nose and flaming red hair?" lied Hank.

Jeremy looked blank. "Oh right, yes, Timothy. Okay, see you later." And off he went.

"Freckles?" whispered Annie when they were out of earshot. "What *are* you talking about?"

"Luckily, Ace, Mr Hatcliff is one of life's talkers – not one of its listeners."

Hank smiled and went to the bar to order a sarsaparilla. The barman said he didn't stock it and was amazed when Hank pointed to a bottle on a shelf. Hank watched the puzzled look on the barman's face. He really was beginning to enjoy himself.

CHAPTER THIRTEEN

... AND DOWN THE ALLEY

THE WEDDING reception was almost over and people were starting to drift off home. Hank had mingled and spoken with a lot of guests over the course of the evening but had only got one more piece of information.

He overheard guests complimenting Kieran Smith on the way he'd tackled the thieves as they'd seen the story in the newspaper too. Nothing new there, except that one of them asked him if he was making a habit out of it.

Listening further, Hank learned that Mr Smith had been the first on the scene when a cat burglar some years before had fallen from a high window ledge and died on the street.

"The funny thing was, Kieran," said a guest, who turned out to be a retired policeman, "that the guy who fell off that ledge had no access from the inside of the building. That ledge was the natural way *into* the building he robbed – but an impossible way out. The window was too high up from the floor without a rope and none was found at the scene. I always had a hunch that something was wrong there."

"Wrong, Bill?" Kieran had queried.

"Yeah, and I remembered you were first on the scene. It wasn't my case. None of my business really. And our separate sides of the family were not on speaking terms to say the least. So this is my first chance to 'kick the case around' with you. You see, my guess is that the burglar fell off the ledge after he'd broken the window locks but *before* he'd gotten into the building."

"But the place was completely ransacked," said Kieran

"Yeah," replied the retired cop, "but not by a guy who hadn't even gotten inside the building."

"Well, whodunnit then, Bill?"

"Dunno. Someone lucky perhaps. Lucky enough to stumble into the crime scene – before the crime took place? Maybe he thinks to himself, shame to leave a good crime undone, especially as the 'fall guy' can't tell any different."

They both laughed and were interrupted by other guests chatter.

"Shame you're retired, Bill," thought Hank. "You'd have made a good partner."

Hank mulled over what he'd heard. So, Kieran Smith was first on the scene. Somehow it was doubtful that giving First Aid was on his mind. This case was not the Tony Falco case. But it had a number of similarities, except Tony's body was never found. And Hank knew from Mr Hatcliff's chatter that Smith had been fired for being a suspected thief.

Kieran Smith had spoken to both Hank and Annie briefly but had really been too caught up in family matters to pry too much into the reasons as to why Hank and Annie were there. Besides, he had been distracted by everyone telling him that he was the best dressed guy at the wedding.

Hank watched as Kieran prepared to leave. Hank thought it strange that he was leaving on his own.

He too got to his feet and motioned to Annie to follow.

"Come on, let's see exactly where our friend is going."

Annie was glad to leave. She was soooo bored with the wedding. She *never* wanted to be a grown up, they didn't have any fun at all. All they ever did was talk to one another about the weather; how people looked, and now and then the ladies would pop off to the loo to apply even more make-up to their already heavily made up faces. No thank you!

The night air had grown cold and Hank turned up the collar of his coat. Annie did the same with her jacket. She wished she wasn't wearing a stupid party dress. She felt like a bunch of leaves, rustling as she walked!

It wasn't long before Hank realised where Kieran Smith was going. In the direction of the alleyway! The *City Centre Hotel* was just around the corner from it.

Hank and Annie did their best to keep themselves hidden, without losing sight of the figure just in front. The last thing they wanted was for Smith to know they were following him!

As Hank thought, Smith took a left turn and headed straight for the alleyway. "Now, what business do you have there, Mr Smith?" Hank wondered aloud.

Annie shrugged. "I don't know, Hank, but I'm sure as heck going to find out."

They made their way slowly and stealthily up the alleyway, adjusting their eyes to the even heavier mist that swirled in front of their eyes.

Annie shivered, partly from the cold and partly because she remembered all too vividly what had taken place the last time she had visited the alleyway. She hoped she wouldn't encounter any more coffins that contained nasty surprises!

Despite their best efforts, they lost sight of Kieran Smith. The mist was simply too thick and Hank and Annie were now walking blindly, hoping to somehow come across the man they had been following.

They reached the top of the alleyway, which was now a dead end again, and stopped.

"Where do we go from here?" Annie asked, trying to keep her voice from shaking.

Hank had noticed something strange about the brickwork in the wall next to where he stood. Small shapes seemed to be carved into the bricks. Small, ornate shapes. Some were of tiny little birds, butterflies and other small creatures whilst others were simply curves, triangles and drops. Like raindrops, thought Hank. Or pearls.

He bent to look more closely.

"What is it Hank?" asked Annie. "What do you see?"

"Jewels!" announced Hank. "I see jewels. Look Annie, carved into the brickwork, here, and here, shapes which could easily be made into jewels." He traced one of the curved lines with his finger. "Look, it's like the earring we found. I mean, I know it's not *exactly* like it, but it's the general shape."

He began rubbing other bricks that surrounded the decorated one, brushing away the dust with the sleeve of his coat.

Unexpectedly, the wall began to turn and both were swung straight through to the other side.

Annie was almost knocked off her feet with the suddenness of the movement and she grabbed Hank's arm to steady herself.

The wall stopped turning and Hank and Annie were deposited on the other side.

Hank brushed the dust from his coat. "Well done us!" he said. "Now let's go investigate."

"So," he thought to himself as he and Annie made their way forward, "I *can* walk through walls after all!"

CHAPTER FOURTEEN

THE COFFIN JUNKYARD

HANK couldn't remember afterwards who had fallen first. Himself or Ace? The mist which had been bad enough on the other side of the wall was intensified a million times on this side. They really were walking blindly, so it was little wonder that they fell... straight into a coffin.

It was actually a coffin junkyard that they had stumbled upon. The whole area was full of coffins of all descriptions, half built coffins, coffins without lids, handles for coffins and bottles and bottles of embalming fluid.

Annie was horrified. Her every instinct was to run from this awful place and back to the warmth and cosiness of her bedroom. However, she knew she'd never forgive herself if she didn't find her missing brother.

She tried to get up but her leg was tangled in the belt of Hank's coat. The more they tried to get up and untangle themselves, the worse the situation seemed to get.

Finally, they managed to get up on their feet and climb out of the coffin.

"Over this way," Hank motioned to Annie, pointing in the direction of a heavy wooden door which was the entrance to a large building at the back of the junkyard.

The door creaked loudly when Hank pushed it. Suddenly he found that it was being pulled from the other side. The heavy door swung open and Kieran Smith was standing just inside it. He looked like he'd been expecting Hank and Annie. He turned slowly towards them and gave them a welcoming smile.

Hank said nothing.

"Come in, my friends. I've been expecting you. Took your time solving my little puzzle, didn't you Mr Kane? I thought you'd never work out how to get through the wall. And you call yourself a detective?" He smiled again, a wicked, eerie smile and looked nothing like the Mr Smith they had chatted with not so long ago.

"Oh, I always get there in the end, Kieran, you can count on that," Hank replied.

Smith seemed delighted to talk about what he'd been up to at the wedding. It turned out that he'd been taking photographs of any of the guests who'd been wearing expensive pieces of jewellery. He'd pretended that he'd wanted a shot of them posing with the bride and groom. He'd even managed to make casts of their jewellery by handling it while pretending to admire it.

Next time he saw the jewellery's owner, he would have the copy ready, make some excuse to handle the original and give the owner back the copy without them knowing it! Easy!

He was awaiting the development of some photographs he had taken earlier. He sat down and motioned to his guests to do so, too.

"So, what can I do for you both?" he asked, grinning.

"The small matter of some missing jewels," said Hank. "Not the ones you steal these days, the ones which were taken from a certain Mr Falco some years back. And, oh yes, there's also the small matter of Mr Falco's body?"

Smith laughed.

"And there I was thinking you only wanted your young assistant back. Charlie is it?"

Annie jumped up.

"You have my brother? How dare you? Are you keeping him captive? Let him go!"

Smith motioned to Annie to keep quiet.

"Enough!" he hissed. "You'll see your brother when I'm good and ready. *If* I'm good and ready."

He turned back to Hank. "I'm a great believer in doing deals, Mr Kane. If I give you this, you'll give me that, know what I mean?"

"What kind of deal do you have in mind?" asked Hank sarcastically.

"In return for your young assistant, you're willing to trade... what exactly?"

"This," said Hank, reaching into his pocket and showing Smith the earring.

Smith gasped.

"My great grandmother's earring! Where did you find it? It's been missing for years! It completes the whole set I have. Look, over here." He walked towards a glass case in the centre of the room. Nestling inside, on purple velvet was a matching bracelet, necklace, brooch and one single, solitary earring.

"I have to have it, Kane. It belongs to *my* family, not that bunch of spoilt, rich good for nothings. Give it to me!" he demanded.

"I want to see Charlie," demanded Hank. "No kid, no earring."

Smith thought for a minute then motioned to Hank and Annie to follow him. "This way," he said gruffly, and began to make his way downstairs to a cellar.

Hank and Annie followed. If they had thought the shop upstairs was dark and eerie, it was nothing compared to the cellar that they now found themselves in.

As they went down the wooden stairs they creaked as if in protest. Annie could hear rats scurrying about and felt spiders' webs caught in her hair.

They reached the last step and found themselves in almost total darkness.

Smith again led the way and they followed him, Annie trying not to think of the furry creatures that brushed themselves against her feet as she walked.

She was the first to spot him.

"Charlie!" she cried.

He was bound, gagged and locked in a cage. The walls beside the cage ran with damp and slime and a musty smell hung in the air.

Annie tried to run towards her brother but Smith held her back.

"Wait," he said. "Stand over there. As I said before, no earring, no brother."

Annie looked over at Hank.

"Where's the key?" asked Hank. He was horrified by what he saw but knew that if he lost his cool he'd blow his chances of ever getting Charlie out of here alive.

Smith held out a key.

"Open the cage," instructed Hank.

Smith sighed, but made his way over to the cage. Charlie stared through the bars, wide-eyed. He hadn't been free from the cage since Smith had brought him there.

"So I'm going to lose my promising new assistant," muttered Smith almost to himself as he walked across the cellar floor. "Pity, you have all the makings of a good jeweller, boy. Clever, artistic, bright. Ah well," he sighed, "I'll just have to find someone else."

He turned the key in the lock and told Charlie to come out.

Charlie was weak from lack of food and could barely walk after spending so much time in a cramped position in the cage.

Annie and Hank ran over to support him.

"My earring, Mr Kane. I believe we had a deal," Smith grinned at Hank.

Annie glared at the horrible man. She hoped Hank would keep the earring. He didn't deserve anything after the way he'd treated her brother!

But Hank handed it over. He was a man who was as good as his word. Okay, so he hadn't solved the Falco case, but he'd gotten Charlie back, and that was good enough for now.

As the three made their way up the wooden staircase, Charlie desperately trying to keep on his feet, Smith flicked a switch and plunged the cellar into even deeper darkness.

Hank led the way, trying to feel his way forward, and all the time he could hear Smith laughing from the cellar below.

He reached the top and told Charlie and Annie to follow him as he weaved in and out of the empty coffins which were scattered throughout the room. It was only slightly brighter than the cellar and more often than not Annie fell over a handle or bottle of embalming fluid that was in her way.

It was Charlie, though, who completely lost

his footing and fell headfirst into a coffin. It was a huge coffin which completely swamped him. Hank saw what had happened and turned to help pull him out. "Come on, Charlie," he encouraged. "You can do it."

He gave Charlie his hand and pulled. At the same time, the coffin next to Charlie's began to creak and the lid began to open.

Annie hid behind Hank. She was terrified and this time she didn't care who knew it.

The lid opened completely and out climbed the corpse of Tony Falco.

CHAPTER FIFTEEN

JUDGEMENT DAY

THE CASE was explained in full to the Court of Ghouls. Falco grinned from ear to ear as Hank told them the story of how Falco had, indeed, been crushed by a dustcart and how his body had been hidden by Kieran Smith.

Smith had wanted to get back at the rich side of the family. When he was employed by the Hatcliffs, when he was eighteen or nineteen, he'd seen Falco "casing the joint". He'd realised that Falco was planning to rob the place. He already hated the rich side of the family, who were his employers, so he thought he had the perfect crime.

Tony Falco did the hard bit, took the risk, broke in and got the jewels. Then bingo! Along came Smith with his dust cart and crushed him. Smith had long known about the secret passage into the coffin factory and he hid the dust cart and Tony Falco's body in there before Guy Hatcliff, the owner's son appeared.

Falco had died clutching the jewels with all

his might. And Smith just couldn't get them free! He hadn't intended to keep Falco's body but he just could not get the jewels out of Tony's grip. Even when Falco's body decomposed, such was his soul's desire for the jewels, that even his skeleton would not let go.

Smith had watched as Hank and Charlie scavenged about in the alley. He'd thought that it was only a matter of time before they discovered the secret passage, so he'd tried to kidnap them both but had only managed to get Charlie.

But now, Falco had handed back the jewels and he was forgiven by the Court Of Ghouls. The judge banged his gavel and gave the order for Falco to be allowed into Bandit Heaven.

Tony shook Hank's hand.

"Thanks, Hank, I knew you'd do it."

Hank smiled back. He just wished it was as easy for him to get to the other side. And, though he hadn't used Charlie to help him on this case, he *had* made use of some of the boys from the *Cesspit*. Plus, he *had* used Annie so, really, there was little or no point in him trying to present his case to the Court.

Hank looked with barely concealed disgust at the juror nearest him. He looked as though he had been mauled by a lion, torn from limb to limb, and yet survived the attack. Folds of flesh hung from his face, empty sockets seemed to stare at Hank from where eyes should have been, part of his left arm was eaten away and his right arm looked dangerously gangrenous.

The juror further up the bench was white, the kind of white pallor you only see on dead people. He looked as though all his life blood had been sucked from him, his long, bony fingers stretched out in front of him. His ghostly smile revealed pointed, vampire-like teeth.

Hank looked further up to where the twins sat. Both wore long black leather coats, cropped black hair, cowboy boots and each held a machine gun. Both had horrific burn marks on the sides of their faces and this was the only thing that distinguished one from the other. One was scarred down the right hand side, the other down the left. Their eyes were closed, and their cheeks blistered and wept, pus running down their faces and dripping onto the bench in front of them.

Hank raised his hand. "S'okay guys, I know I don't stand a chance this time. I won't waste your time. Come on, Charlie, Annie, let's get out of here."

The detective and his two young assistants left the court, blinking in the bright moonlight as they pushed open the doors and stood outside.

Charlie stretched. "Boy, it sure is good to be free," he smiled at Hank and Annie.

"Don't mention it, kid," Hank said, patting him on the back. "Things just weren't the same around here without you, now were they Ace?"

Annie walked on in front.

"Oh, I don't know about that," she smiled. "I didn't miss him at all."

"Just one thing, Hank," said Charlie who'd just been hearing most of the case being explained in the court. "Am I right in thinking that *all* the jewels were recovered, even from that case where the cat burglar fell to his death?"

"All the jewels that were declared to the Court Of Ghouls were accounted for."

"But Hank, if Kieran Smith always arranged it so that he was first on the scene, then only *he* knows what jewels were around..."

"Excuse me, kid, but you aint thinking," said Hank.

"What do you mean?" asked Charlie, looking puzzled.

"Well, who was first on the scene when Falco died and when that cat burglar died?" asked Hank.

"Kieran Smith of course!" said Charlie.

"Wrong, kid."

"Well who then?"

Just then, TG came into view, having just crossed over on to Buchannan Street. Charlie turned to Hank. He looked like he'd just worked it out. Hank put his hand up. Charlie had learnt that this gesture usually meant only one thing. Don't say another word.

"One day..." whispered Hank to Charlie, "...one fine day, I'll put him away."

"That's one case you can solve on your own," whispered Annie.

"Did I miss your hearing, Hank?" said TG, as he joined them. "My, that was over quickly, wasn't it? Well you're still here. So no need to ask how it went. Sorry Hank. Looks like we have a few more cases to solve, huh!"

"At least one more TG, at least one," smirked Hank, wondering if he'd finally met his match.

look very strange. The police, after forensic tests, have the body buried. Is this really the end of Hank Cane? It will be, unless Charlie can work out Hank's secret code in the letter in his desk drawer, marked "ONLY TO BE OPENED IN AN EMERGENCY". If this isn't an emergency what is? But can Charlie handle all the secrets in the letter?

THE CORPSE THAT SANG

A Corpse seen in 1940's Los Angeles turns up in 2002, singing on TV! The strangest coincidence – or is Hank's old flame haunting him. She was a great detective who ended up in Sleuth Heaven – so, why give that up just to sing? Charlie sees the romantic side of Hank and wants to throw up! How can they solve cases with Hank staring at the TV all night? For the first time, Charlie has to take the calls at Hank's office. At last, the Kid can prove his worth, and he resolves to break the case of *The Corpse That Sang*.

THROW AWAY THE KEY

"Help me... please, help me!" A voice identifying itself only as "The Prisoner" keeps calling Hank's phone, pleading for help. Despite being asked why, the panicking voice just keeps calling. Charlie introduces Hank to the latest technology in phone tapping and they listen carefully to the background noises, searching for clues. They get worried when they begin to recognise some sounds, which are too familar for comfort. The Prisoner is very, very close to home!!

GHOST CAR 49

The siren from an old-fashioned American police car is heard echoing around the streets at night. The sound of screeching tyres, blaring police radio, 1940s jazz music and constant gunfire freak out the local residents. Needless to say, Charlie gets the call: " Better get over here, Kid. Looks like we've got something." But how will they bring Car 49 to a halt? And who is at the wheel?!

THE DEAD DETECTIVE SERIES

www.booksnoir.com

www.deaddetective.com

Hey guys! Hank Kane here. Check out my website www.deaddetective.com *to keep up to date with my interactive e-book* Web of Intrigue, *an internet adventure where you, the reader, can help me on the case.*

P.S. You'd better be good!